DWAYNE'S BIG DECISION

JACKSON JEFFREY

Illustrated by Alegria and Omayra Michael

Young Authors Publishing

Young Authors Publishing
www.youngauthorspublishing.org

Book Design by April Mostek

Our books may be purchased in bulk
for promotional, educational, or business use.
Please contact Young Authors Publishing by email at
info@youngauthorspublishing.org.

DEDICATION

I dedicate this book to my mom and dad, Chenika and Robert Jeffrey. Thank you for always believing in me!

"You made the winning shot, Dwayne!" my teammate said. Yes, that's me making the game-winning shot. I love playing basketball. I've been playing since I was 10.

I also play the French horn, but I keep that a secret.

I've always had a passion for basketball, and I'm really good, too! I've been team captain for two years.

During class I focus on the new plays when finally, the bell rings. "Dwayne, can I talk to you for a second? I talked to your mom and she said you're really good at French horn—you should consider joining the band," my teacher says.

"Okay, I'll think about it," I reply, running to basketball practice.

Finally, school ends and I run to basketball practice, where all my friends are already on the court doing warm-ups.

"Pass the ball, I'm open!" one of my teammates shouts. I watch my teammate come from up the court and a defender rush to cover him. I make eye contact with the net and take the shot.

Swish! It goes in with ease!

"Let's go back to Dwayne's house and shoot some hoops before dinner!"

All my friends pile into my mom's car, and we spend the afternoon laughing, talking, and shooting shots until slowly people begin to rush home for dinner.

"Have you thought about what your teacher said?" Mom questions.

"Yes I have, but I don't want to join," I say firmly.

"Just go and try it out, and if you're sure you don't like it, I won't make you do it."

I was nervous to go to band practice after school. I didn't know anyone, and this was my first time missing basketball practice.

"Hi—my name is Tyler, and you must be Dwayne! You can sit next to me in practice!" Tyler beamed.

Band practice was super fun. We did ice-breakers, and I got to meet everyone, and they were super cool! I met a lot of new people and we even went to go get pizza afterward!

"Mom, I had so much fun today! I really want to join, but I don't want my friends to make fun of me," I cry.

"I told you it would be fun. You should join—and don't worry about what others think. If they're your real friends, they'll understand," my mom says, kissing my head.

After my conversation with my mom, I decide to join the band. I start splitting my time between basketball and band practices. When I start bringing my French horn to class, my teammates begin to make fun of me, each of them dissing me. "You're such a nerd!"

"I can't believe you joined band."

"You can't be a nerd and play basketball."

By the time class starts, I'm mad at all my friends for being so insensitive.

"You're such a nerd, like, get a life."

"You can't be a nerd *and* play basketball—you have to pick one!"

"Why don't you go do some homework."

At lunch, my basketball friends won't let me sit with them, so I wander the cafeteria until my band friends invite me to join them. I decline because I don't want to choose between my band friends and my basketball friends, so I sit alone … which is even worse!

I see a crowd start to form, and look over at my teammate making fun of the band members. This is when I've had enough of the bullying!

"Why are you over here? You nerds have to sit in the back of the cafeteria," my teammate says, pushing Tyler.

"You guys don't have to be mean to each other! We're all doing what we love to do and that's what's important. It shouldn't matter what anyone thinks as long as you're happy with yourself!" I say.

After I finish, I ask my old friends and my new friends to sit together.

Slowly, everyone agrees. Before long, everyone is talking and laughing, and many friendships are being formed.

Yes, that's me, playing my French horn solo. I love playing basketball and I love the French horn. All my friends accept me for who I am, and I always remember to do what I love, regardless of what anyone thinks.

ABOUT THE AUTHOR

Jackson Jeffrey lives in Atlanta, GA. He loves to play basketball and the French horn. He also loves attending Ebenezer Baptist Church; all the members and staff are always so loving! When he grows up, he wants to be a professional basketball player and an entrepreneur.

ABOUT YOUNG AUTHORS PUBLISHING

We believe that all kids are story-worthy!

Young Authors Publishing is a not-for-profit children's book publisher that exists to share the stories of children, many who live in underrepresented communities. Young authors participate in our Experience Program where they are paired with a trained writing mentor who helps them write their children's book. Once their manuscript is complete, young authors learn the fundamentals of financial literacy, entrepreneurship and public speaking. When you purchase a book from Young Authors Publishing, you're helping a child write a new story and change the narrative.

OUR FAVORITE PART!

Eighty percent of all the book royalties are deposited into a secured savings account for each young author to use toward their post-secondary plans.

Learn more about our impact at www.youngauthorspublishing.org